GW00375037

This is a story of jealousy, a man who would seem to have everything,
but the one thing he doesn't have jealousy takes over, he finds away to
destroy the man who has what he wants.

But things turn out far worse for him, then what he could ever had
imagined, years after he had done this terrible deed, he has been found
out. He does not understand why his world has been torn apart.

Acknowledgments

And a big thanks to

Tess Beane

Kerry Marshall

Best wishes
I C Henshe

Just deserts

Chapter 1

THE STORY STARTS with John just moving into his hired room, a dirty smelly, small room at the lower end of the market on the outskirts of the town. He had been a successful private eye. His detective agency had been built up over a number of years. He was middle aged, an ex soldier and he had built his company after he retired from the army; he had been in the army from leaving school so he knew nothing else. He had just broken up with his wife, who he had been married for a number of years

John is in his late fifties, he had been successful in running his own detective business, so why was he in this rented room? John looked around; it looked as if it not been decorated since it had been built. The wall paper was dark from the cigarette stains. The light was dull, the bulb wattage not strong enough for a room that size.

As he sat on the edge of the bed, with his head in his hands he started to sob. He asked himself how did this happen? What have I …done I've lost it all and I don't know why? (*Just then the door opened*)

"Are you settled in then" Raymond walked into the room; he is the landlord a dirty untidy man similar age to John. It would appear that he does not see many people to talk to, so when he does he likes to chat a lot, and find out all he can about them.

"I think it will take some getting used to (*trying to get some muck off his trouser leg from the bed*) I hope this does not stain"

"Don't get grumpy with me…this room is much sought after, anyway how are you here? You look like a well to do type, you can call me Raymond or Ray whatever's easier. That's my name, I don't usually get involved with my tenants but you look as if you could do with a friend

"It's a bit of a long story"

"That's all right, come down stairs and we will have a cuppa. *(Raymond gets up)* Speed up man; I would like a cuppa today if that's possible"

"I don't know, I mean I'm not sure if I'd be good company"

"Don't be silly, get it off your chest man and you'll feel better"

John starts to stand up still unsure if he should or shouldn't. "I suppose it won't do any harm"

"I'll tell you what I'll bring the drinks up here, won't be long" Raymond goes and John sits back down on the bed.

After a short time John walks around the room, he picks up his bag and starts to empty it on the bed "What a shit hole its worse than a pigsty, what a fucking hovel ([*Raymond walks back into the room, with a tray with two cups and some biscuits on a small plate, he glares at John*) Sorry…but I…err I'm not used to people living like this"

"Never mind, I should decorate some time; Hurry…the tea is almost ready; do you want a biscuit with yours?"

"I had my own private eye company (*John says smugly*) I was making loads of money I was turning jobs down I was doing really well"

"So how is it that you are here then? I mean to say no matter what has happened you must be able to afford a hotel or something"

"That's the bitter pill, I was asked to take on this case, this man rang me, out of the blue one day, asked me to meet up with him, so I did, and he was in a right state…"

"What do you mean in a right state? Had he been beaten up?"

"No! No I mean crying…anyway I listened to his story, and took on his case"

"So you end up a broken down man yourself, were there gangsters? And did they beat the two of you up, I don't want any trouble
(*Raymond gets up and looks out of the window*) here…I think that it might be better that you go"

"No… Sorry for snapping but what I should have said…was that… there were no gangsters or any violent behaviour just me being conned out of my…life…my living my livelihood"

"What do you mean...your life…?"

"Yes they took every…damn thing… that had ever meant anything to me… so yes they took my life…the life that I knew"

"They… you said they. Who are they? This man that rang you…was he the reason?"

"It was in a pub when I first met up with …Wayne…Wayne was is name or is his name; I really don't know now if that was his name"

"If you're a detective is there no way finding out? I'm sure if someone took all I have (*pointing to the room*) I would find a way to know who and why they had done this to me, sometimes it's good just to talk about it you never know, you might find the answer"

"I don't know? I've gone over it and over it in my head and can't find the reason why or how someone would do this"

"Maybe tell someone who's not involved, you might find something you've missed"

John sat on the edge of the bed thinking if he should or shouldn't, then he said ok he would start from the beginning.

Chapter 2

The first meeting

"LIKE I SAID I had this phone call I, had a lot of work on so I didn't really want to do this job, but some how he persuaded me" He then started to tell Raymond the story and reliving it again.

Wayne was in the bar area first, he went to the barman and asked if there was a well dressed man. Assuming that John would be in a suit and most of those who were there were in ordinary clothes.

John came in nearly at the same time. He looked around but not wanting to go up to anyone, as there were three others in the bar area. So John ordered himself a drink. Wayne approached John from behind, with a tap on the shoulder.

"Hello… are you John?"

"Yes …you must be…" He paused; he had learnt from past experience it was best not to give a stranger any name, until they had given it themselves. They might not be the person, who he was supposed to be meeting.

"Wayne (*he said as he stuck out his hand to shake Johns hand*) Can we sit over there (*They go and sit at a table*) I rang you, my name is…Wayne…I work for this big company, my wife works for the same one but more on the office side of things. I'm on the board, but…the company I am part of, it's worth almost ten million"

"So how can I help you? What is it that is worrying you?"

"It's my wife I think she is having an affair, with the head of the company"

"So do you want me to get… sorry find the evidence (*John's phone starts to ring*) It's the wife… I will take it across here…(*John walks away into a quiet corner*)Yes I am…I'm with a client now; I think this will be a good earner he is loaded, yes… yes dear … if you let me get a word in… no I am not getting cantankerous…sorry…sorry… yes…yes ok I will see you later… I am going to make a good bit money out of this one, let me get my hands on this…ok see you later, love you bye (*he heads back to Wayne*) Look Wayne I have just turned a job down, I can see that you are in need of some help, so if you can get me some details, a photo of your wife, one of the man that you think she is having an affair with, time and location that you think they will be at (*Wayne hands John a photo*) Is this your wife?"

"Yes…it is, sorry she is…"

"She looks stunning, is she a model? (*Wayne shakes his head*) I will get onto it straight away; do you have a contact number?"

"It's on the bottom of that notepaper, I'll go now… back to work…do you know … anything but… this… (*He said in a heartbroken way*) Do you not want her name?"

"No it sometimes makes it harder, you sometimes slip out the name and they wonder how you know them. So I never get the name of the target, do you know if she is meeting him tonight and maybe what place it would be…or… it just saves a lot of time and expense for you"

"She sometimes comes in here after work so if you stay here she might not be too long, I overheard her saying she was popping in for a drink I'll go, should not be too long to wait" Wayne heads to the exit, he stopped then turned away, then stood for a short time, as if he is still uncertain if he is doing the right thing.

John takes out his phone "Hello, I've taken on this case, I'm going to go or might be going to a wine bar (*not wanting to tell her where he was*)…no I'm working….I might be late depending on what happens. See you later, don't ring me I will ring you when it is convenient…bye"

Wayne's wife walks in, Sally is laughing she is talking to an older gentleman. They go to a table with some drinks. He's flirting with her and she's flirting with him. John takes his phone from the table to take a photo of her with this man, who she seems to be friendly with.

John cannot believe how beautiful she is, how sexy she looks, not just her body, her cloth's made her look a million dollars, it was everything about her, even her personality. Just as he took the photo someone walked passed in front of him, "No way!" he said out loud, some people turning looking towards him. He was disappointed, it would have been a great photo from the position he was sitting, it could have looked as if she might have been kissing him.

Sally also turned her head towards John, she smiled and got up then she went towards John, holding her wineglass half-full with red wine, as she got near John she stumbled towards him and spilled her drink onto him.

"Sorry I wasn't watching where I was going" she then started to wipe his chest.

"No just leave it, it will be ok! It's an old shirt it's ready for the bin anyway"

"I'm Sally; I must at least buy you a drink"

"No…no you're all right. Like I said it's an old one and ready for the bin"

"Would you like to sit down over there and join us? I will pay for your shirt to get dried cleaned"

"D…don't be silly tell you what, we'll have a drink together and call it evens"

They move over to the table where Sally was sitting with her friend, her friend made an excuse to leave and the two of them sit down, John pulls out a chair for her, this goes down well she gives him a lovely smile.

"What are you doing here? I have never seen you in here before?

"I've just called in on my way home, I was passing and thought I would come in, have a look how the other half live. Would you like a refill?"

"I would love one, if you are having one with me? (*She pushes her empty glass over towards John*) Unless you don't want one with me"

"Yes I would love to have one with you. Aren't you stopping long?

"Not much longer, I am waiting for my husband to come and pick me up"

"What time is he picking you up? He's not the jealous type is he?"

"When I ring him…. I should ring him shortly he'll be wondering what I'm up too. No he's a kitten I love him very much"

"I just have to make a call myself, excuse me and I will be soon back, (*he rings Wayne and tells him that she's going to call him shortly*) Don't let her know that you know me…right ok …try and let me have a little more time to get to know her, (*he then heads back to the table*) Have you rung your husband?"

"No not yet I'm enjoying myself, are you not? (*She looks down at her empty glass then her eyes turn up towards John with a smile*) Are we having that drink sir?"

"John…John is my name and yes… I have not had this much fun for a long time" he says pulling his wet shirt off his chest.

"I think you are probably right, I should give Wayne a call or text. (*She then takes her phone out from her little handbag, not mush bigger than a purse*) Are we not having a drink then?" (Picking her glass up again)

John picks up the glasses from the table, asks her what sort of wine it was, and then heads to the bar, when he's there he turns back towards the table, he can see that Sally is on her phone, he gets the drinks reasonably quick, he takes no time to get back to the table placing her drink in front of her with a smile.

"Will he be long? Your husband, is he far from here?" Sally receives a text.

"No he's out and about. He said he'll be about five minutes" she places her hand on Johns he grabs hold of it and kiss's it.

"Sorry…sorry I don't know what came over me"

Wayne enters the room, John sees him and pulls his hand away from Sally who had not moved, with a smile she stands up and kisses Wayne on the cheek.

"This is my charming husband Wayne; sorry I don't remember your name?"

"John...Yes my name is John"

Wayne sticks out his hand to shake John's; John stands up and takes hold of Wayne's hand.

"Sorry that we can't stop... I'm parked on a double yellow line, we'll see you again some time maybe? Right Sally you ready?"

"Maybe tomorrow night I'm in around about this time most evenings"

She blows John a kiss, Wayne is unaware what she has done. John did the same back to her, then he sat back down, with a great big smile on his face. And feeling superior about himself, he was sitting ever so smugly.

Chapter 3

JOHN GOT BACK HOME his wife Jan is in the living room watching some programme on TV. She is a cool person, not much affection towards anyone. Unless it was in her favour,

"Well how did it go? Your meeting with God knows who"

John was now in the kitchen looking for something to eat; Jan could hear him looking in the cupboards, but sat watching her programme,

"Well it's hard to tell on the first meeting, is there anything to eat? I'm starving"

"Look in the fridge, I have left your dinner in there, just put it into the microwave, come and see what's on the telly (*John comes back and gets into the chair, just to the side of Jan*) Tell you who I was talking to today, that young lad who does the advertisement on the telly. The one with …you never believe this I can't remember, He's a lovely lad, he's called Frank (*John eating*) I think we are having a drink with him and his girlfriend tomorrow (*John started to fall asleep in the chair*) John…John…JOHN!" Jan shakes John until he wakes up.

"Sorry it's been a long day…you said something about a drink?"

"Yes tomorrow, with that young actor from the telly around 11am, that's if you can make it"

"I will have to look in my diary… I'm sure that I have something to do"

"You had better cancel it... hadn't you it's no good me telling people how wonderful you are and they never meeting you is it, what are they going to think of me?"

Jan turns her back on John; John puts his plate on the small table next to him, then goes over towards her and puts his arms around her.

"I can't just call things off, just to keep you...your friends' happy can I? After all I have work to do. Come on turn around, come on" Jan turns around.

"You do as I tell you. You just remember who the boss is. Or do I have to remind you" She smiles softly and kisses him on the cheek, he smiles

"Yes dear, I know who the boss is, but you remember who the breadwinner is and who keeps you in the lifestyle that you are used too"

Jan tries another way to win him round. She puts her arms around his shoulders a gives him a kiss on the lips.

"Will you try and come? I would like you to meet them, even if it's just a short time please...please, you never know you might like them"

"Look what I'll do is...I'll be honest I don't know what I'll be doing, you know I have to take the time to follow the client, they make all the decisions, I can't just say you stay there until I get back and don't do anything that might give evidence as I will miss it. And won't be able to prove that you're the scumbag that your partner thinks you are"

"If you can I would be ever so grateful, I tell everyone about you, how wonderful you are, and what a super husband I have"

Chapter 4

Back in John's room

"BLOODY HELL I wasn't expecting all of that, that's a lot going on, by the sounds of it you must have had a thing going on with her, was she as beautiful as you said? Sound's like she's a model"

"She wasn't a model but yes she could have been. She had…has everything going for her, that first time I saw her she looked like she had just walked out of a glossy magazine or something"

"How do you become to be a spy?"

"Secret agent that's what I am a secret agent"

"Well a secret agent then. What sort of things did you do? I mean it's not just affairs is it"

"No not at all, it's all sort of things, business mostly"

"Like this one that's ruined you, was it the boss? He found out that you had something on him and that woman…Sally I think you said? And he got the first kick in"

Raymond walked to the window, looked out then back to his chair in the corner of the room. John just looked at him it was something that Raymond had said, as much as he would not admit to anyone Raymond might have something with that comment.

"I don't think so; there's more to it than meets the eye,

"Like what? You take on this case then you end up broke, it's as simple as that I would say"

Raymond starts to pick up the cups and puts them on a tray. He looks at John who has his head in his hands, clearly trying to work things out.

"Look if you want you can come down to my room, it's bigger than this and the seats are more comfortable, only if you want and we can put the kettle on again, if you like, I don't know about you but I'm thirsty"

Raymond heads towards the door, one hand holding the tray and the other holding the door handle. He turned back towards John; John was still holding his head in his hands.

"I'm going. If you change your mind just come down and give me a knock, it's on the bottom floor the first door on the right when you come in the front door, or on the left if you look at the front door, you'd be surprised how many knock on the wrong door, not that you'll get an answer, nobody's in that room just now, they are away for a few days… back on… they are back tonight, I just remembered or is it tomorrow morning? I think"

He stood there for a moment trying to remember if it was tonight or in the morning, not that it would matter one way or another. Just he did not want to be seen telling or giving the wrong information.

"Like I said if you want" Raymond then went out and shut the door behind himself, he waited just outside the door for a short time to see if John would follow, but he could not hear anything in the room, no sound of John moving, so he headed down the stairs with his tray and cups, and most importantly his biscuits.

John sat for a moment thinking what he should do? He came to the conclusion that Raymond seemed to be a sensible man, an intelligent man so it might not do any harm talking to him.

He followed Raymond down the staircase, Raymond was one flight below him, Raymond could hear John on the squeaky staircase, some of the floorboards were not screwed down properly so they squeaked when walked on, from each squeak Raymond knew more or less where John was, Raymond had lived there all his adult life, so he knew that John had decided to come down after him, so he slowed down a little so that John could catch up with him, because if John did not see where or which room he was going to go into, John could easily bypass it. And end up down in the cellar and Raymond did not want anybody down there.

They got into Raymond's room, Raymond put the kettle on straight away, got the cups then John without being asked got on with his story.

Chapter 5

JOHN GOT HIMSELF comfortable in one of Raymond's chairs, then started with the story, he explained that some parts he wasn't present so he would just have to fill them in as he seen it. Raymond nodded his head to accept that was ok, so he started when he was supposed to see this actor, the parts he wasn't there was what his wife had told him sometime later.

John explained that it they had arranged to meet in a coffee bar

"Did John not fancy coming then?" Frank asked as he was pulling a chair out for Jan.

"No he was still in bed; he was working late; he even fell asleep whilst eating his tea" They laugh Frank then put his hand over Jan's she half pulled away then stopped.

"Why did you pull away then stop? Do you not feel what I feel?"

She then pulls her hand away "No we shouldn't"

"We shouldn't what? Do what our heart tells us...why not, Jan I think that you're mad... staying with a man that can't... NO a man that does not see how you should be taken care of"

"He does take care of me, he takes good care of me, he works long hours, it's...how it always been"

"Ok I shouldn't interfere"

"I think that I should go..." She half gets up then she paused

"No…please I'm sorry… did I tell you that I might be playing a part in a new play?

She sits back down, she loves to watch a play, so she was interested straight away" No what type of play?"

"It's a love story… I play a part of a gigolo, you know… I think I can do with some help…you might be able to help, if that is alright?"

"How can I help? I know nothing about acting"

"It's a kissing part…you know that I'm shy and not had a lot of…girlfriends"

"I would never have guessed. The way you flirt with me"

"You make me feel alive… when I'm with you I feel I could do almost anything; you know what I mean I …"

Jan interrupts Frank "Frank you must stop this, how could I help?"

"Like I said it's a kissing part, you could show me how it's done with passion" as he said this he put his hand on hers and the other hand rubs her cheek.

"No…No Frank I think you have to stop this silly behaviour, you have to understand I am married and I love John a great deal" She stands up again as if to leave.

"Jan …Jan comeback…right I'm sorry, but there is a part that might interest you. (*Jan sits down*) Right it's this part that I'm in and I have to get this woman into bed, for a bet, anyway that part could be yours if you are interested"

"How sorry am I. A bet! Do you think that I'm that kind of woman; do I come across like some sort of desperate housewife?"

"It's the story in the play; no I don't think you're that sort of lady at all. All you would be doing is a part in the play. Playing a part that's all"

"I mean what would I have to do? Who would I have to talk to? Would I need a ... You know what you call them ...you know what I mean. A... an ...agent?"

"An agent?"

"Yes...yes an agent, would I need one of them?"

"Well it would be better if you had one I guess, but there's always a way around that. Do you want me to call my agent, or you could have a word with my agent yourself, but if all else fails we will get around it some way. This is excellent, it's only a small part but it would be wonderful if you would be in it. I could speak to my agent later today, and see what he can do for you, I know that he says his books are full but I'm sure that he could squeeze you in for this small part"

"Do you think so? I would love to give it a go, it must be so exciting acting I've got butterflies in my stomach just thinking about it"

"Calm down you haven't got the part yet, you still have to audition for it. But I see no reason why you could not do it. And you're right I think everyone gets those butterflies. It's so exciting going for the position, then if you get it well...you will see how I feel"

"When do you think it will be? And can you tell me anything about it or...I'm so thrilled I feel like jumping in the air, thank you… (*She then gets up and goes around to Franks side of the table, then kisses him on the cheek*) thank you! But I must go now, you've got me all excited, don't forget to call"

"Jan …Jan comeback… see you later"

John's back in the room with Raymond, his head back in his hands clearly thinking and trying to work things out.

"That's all I know about that meeting"

"Did she get the part? Well I never film actors and secret agents I'll be able to dine out on this for a good long while (*Raymond then got up clearing the cups away*) what about that other girl you mentioned before did you not see her again?"

"Well funnily enough I did, it was later that day as it happens"

They both sit down again and John tells the story as he remembered it.

Chapter 6

"WE HADEN'T ARRANGED to meet up in the park. I rang Sally when Jan was meeting this actor… bloke? Frank. Anyway we got talking and she mentioned something about going to the park, when we were in the park sitting on a bench. Sally s head was on my shoulder it was lovely"

"This is lovely I feel so well-matched with you and it feels so right, how did you know I would be here?"

"I don't know, I just thought you looked like a person… that liked the fresh air" John turned towards her, had she forgotten that she had told him about the park?"

"I often come here in the summer, its good seeing the children run around, the parents chasing the little ones around …playing football…you know things like that"

"Yes it must be good I suppose. Do you have children?"

"No Wayne never had time, or the want for them…do you…I mean have children"

"No the wife never liked the idea"

"Do you…did you ever want children?"

"Once I did but now… I think I've missed the chance"

"Never say never" John brushes her hair away from her face and kisses her; she cuddles into him, as they sit for a moment she then pulls John onto her as she falls back into the park bench.

"I wish that I had met you years ago; you are perfect"
Sally says as she cuddles into John, then John's phone starts to ring.

"I will have to answer it… its work" he moves away with his back towards Sally, in the meantime Sally texts someone.

"Was it important?" Sally asks with a smile.

"No but I will have to go …What are you up to later?"

"Don't know Wayne said he might be going for a drink…why?"

"I…I…would like to take you out…I think you know why"

Sally's phone starts to ring, John gets up to give her some privacy but stays near enough to hear what's being said.

"Yes Wayne… all night well that's not on! (*She hangs up with a face like thunder, then turns to John*) That was Wayne, yes …yes… I would like to go for a drink with you later, Wayne says that he might be out all night, a lads night out he says"

"Will I pick you up or… will I meet you somewhere?"

"Yes you can come and pick me up, from home… thanks that's a good idea John, I would like that, what time would you like me to be ready?"

"Around seven...seven thirty, if that's ok?"

Sally scribbles her address on some paper "Here is my address; I will be ready and waiting, don't be late"

Chapter 7

JOHN IS SITTING back in the room with Raymond. Head in his hands

"Well ...well what happened next... was that her husband on the phone?"

"To be honest, not sure who it was, but this is when things went really crazy (*his face tells Raymond that he is still trying to work out what happened*) I just don't know what went wrong"

"Come on man, you just can't stop halfway and say you don't know, I think you do know!"

"I tell you, I can't...I cannot work out what went on after my next meeting with Sally; next thing I know is...I'm out on my ear"

"Think hard man, you will work it out, if you stop and look at it in a different way, what was your next meeting?"

"Well I got to her flat a little early, so I decided to give her a call...I keep asking myself what possessed me to go to her flat? Well I guess I thought I could have learned a lot, about her"

"So you went to her flat? What happened?"

"Yes I went in and what happened was...was...I suppose strange"

"So what happened? God! It's like standing over wet paint, waiting for it to dry"

"Well I got to her flat, I knocked on the door, got no answer, I tried again, still no answer"

"So what happened?"

"I was just about to go, then the door opened...swung open, no one was there... I walked in; there was a light in the back of the building...I guess that was where the bathroom was"

John was standing looking towards the light, just then the door opened, out came Sally with a towel around her.

"What are you doing?" She then dropped her towel, giving John an eyeful.

"Sorry the door was open (*still standing looking at her naked body*) lets cover you up (*he picks up a dressing gown, which was lying over a chair the same time Sally is picking her towel up from the floor and wrapping it around herself*) You will catch your death standing like that"

He then covers her shoulders and kisses her on the cheek, she puts her arms around him and they kiss passionate, the towel dropping from under her dressing gown to the floor.

"No...No stop please! I think you might have the wrong idea"

"What! But...I thought you"

Sally interrupts him before he could say anything else.

"WHAT ON EARTH... DO YOU THINK YOU ARE DOING!?"

She then slapped him, the door opened and in came Wayne, by this time she had the towel back on.

"Oh hello again John…what's going on here? I think me and you need to have a talk don't you"

"It's not what it looks like"

"Of course it's not, I've just come in and you have your tongue down my wife's neck…her towel on the floor"

Back in Raymond's room there's not a lot said, between John and Raymond, John then tells Raymond that when Wayne had cone back home early. He had found himself in a very embarrassing position so he left quickly. Raymond nodded and said that he bet he did, "you left early…with a smile" John then starts to tell him about the next meeting.

Chapter 8

The coffee shop

UNKNOWN TO JOHN a few days later Wayne had purposely met his wife Jan. Jan had been shopping and stopped off for a coffee, she had arranged to meet up with someone and was waiting when Wayne walked in, he tripped on one of Jan's shopping bags. Jan was sitting with a number of shopping bags near her feet.

"Sorry I did not see you; I hope I haven't broken anything"

Jan was looking in her bag "No it looks ok"

"Can I get you another drink?"

"No you're all right" she said wafting her hand towards him

"Go on please I feel a right fool"

Jan looked him up and down "Well I suppose…go on then, I still have a little time before I get picked up" Wayne then sat down next to her and ordered two drinks from the waitress.

"I'm really sorry about tripping over your bag, by the way my name is Wayne" he said as his hand went across the table to shake hers.

"Pleased to meet you, I'm called Jan" she did not lift her hand to meet his; she even looked away as she said this.

The waitress took no time to bring the drinks; she placed them down on the table then went on her way, before she asked if there was anything else they wanted, they both said no almost at the same time, which made them laugh. This was a good ice breaker; Wayne took no time in trying to find similar things that they could talk about.

"I'm supposed to be shopping myself, but took time out to rest"

"No stamina, that's the problem with men, they look in one shop and think that's it"

"It's the lights"

"What?"

"The lights, the shop lights, they hurt most men's eyes"

"That's the most ridiculous thing I've ever heard, lights hurt men's eyes" Jan starts to laugh out loud as she turns away waving her hand towards him as if to dismiss him.

"No it's a scientific fact...most men can't stand the bright lights, that are in most shops"

"You're a typical man, any excuse...what's the reason for not washing dishes? The soap burns (*sarcastic*) you tell us anything...you must think we've just got off the banana boat" They both laugh.

"Can I get you a bun ...or something to eat (*he asks her as he starts to stand*) I'm starving I can't eat by myself...so will you be so kind and join me?"

"Be so kind to join me, really! No I think I should be going not..." Just then the door opens and in comes John, the look of horror on his face seeing Wayne sitting talking to his wife. Jan just turned her head to see John coming into the room, she gave him a big warm smile and a wave to get his attention.

"This is my husband (*holding her hand out to meet John*) this is   Wayne...I'm right aren't I?"

"Yes you are" Wayne stands up putting his hand out to meet John's hand.

"Sorry I am ever so forgetful...with names" Jan says as John sits near Jan, with the look of fear on his face.

"Sorry I did not catch your name" Wayne says as his hand reaches across the table, John's hands meets Wayne's, Johns arm is quivering.

"Don't be so nervous, he's not going to bite you silly" Jan says laughing the way John seems to be shaking.

"Sorry John...John is my name" John says still shaking; worried that Wayne might have or might say something to Jan which would take some explaining.

"I'm Wayne, me and your charming wife, are having an affair"
 Jan and Wayne giggle.

"Don't tell him that he'll believe you...are you not going to order anything from the counter John?"

"So how do you two know each other? (*John asks with a slight stutter*) my wife moves in certain circles, I can't keep up with her"

"Well believe it or not I've just bumped into you wife, I knocked one of her shopping bags over and thought it only right to have a drink with her, and a bite to eat"

"Ever so clumsy… he did (*shaking her head*) knock my shopping bags over, we've got to be on our way shortly, but it was nice meeting you …Wayne?" She asks still unsure of his name

"Yes it is, nice seeing you both, are you not going to have that bun with me? They do a good jam and cream bun here I hear"

"No we must be on our way you know how it is, and I've parked on a double yellow line and I thought I saw a traffic warden on his way, so best not stop"

"Yes I know how it is, I'm certain no doubt we'll meet again in the near future" Wayne sticks his hand out to John, John sticks his hand out slowly, they shake hands, Johns hand is being squeezed hard and being stopped him leaving, until Jan turned her head. Then Wayne lets John's hand go. John and Jan turn and walk to the exit. Just as they are about to leave Jan stops.

"Yes we will stop and have that bun with you"

"But Jan we have thing's to do"

"They can wait there's nothing that will spoil or can't wait…well apart from moving the car from the yellow lines" she laughs again.

John goes out to move the car, Wayne orders the buns, they have tea and a bun each; Wayne gets a phone call just as the order arrives, he has to leave. But he waits until John comes back.

"Sorry I have to go something has popped up and … well you know how it is; we will have to do this again sometime"

"Yes no doubt" John says in a squeaky voice.

"Jan did you know your husband... (*Jan looks up towards Wayne*) no it doesn't matter, see you again sometime... John!" Wayne leaves the building, but just before his exit, he turns with a menacing look towards John.

"He is charming man, don't you think so (*John still memorised by the look he received didn't hear Jan*)...John ...John are you not listening to me?"

"Sorry dear, I was deep in thought for a moment"

"Well you should pay attention... and stop staring (*John was still staring at the doorway*) I wont tell you again stop...stop now!"

"Sorry dear I thought I knew him from somewhere, never mind was just trying to work it out"

"You're losing the plot I worry about you at times"

"What... what do you mean losing the plot?"

John looked down towards the floor, when he looked back up he's back in Raymond's room.

Chapter 9

"SO DO YOU think he followed your wife? Or was he in cahoots with her?"

"I never thought of that, she might have been! I wonder?" John starts rubbing his chin as he's walking around the room.

Then there is a knock at the door, Raymond gets up, he asks John to wait he would be only a moment. John can hear Raymond talking but can not see who or make out what they are talking about; there is a lot of muttering. Raymond enters the room again.

"Was that important? I'll go if you like"

"No you stay, just someone who wants to see you"

"Who? Nobody knows that I'm here"

"John...do...you know...no I can't say...well better not say"

"What...what can't you say?"

"Well the bloke that's gone upstairs... he knows you and you know him" Footsteps can be heard going up the stairs, then again come back down. Just then a man bursts into the room holding something in his hand,

"This is Len"

"I know that, he's my brother!" John says with a confused expression on his face.

"Well how are you doing?" Len asked with a straight face

"Well it's not the Ritz is it" John replied with arrogance in his voice.

"It got me back on my feet that's right isn't it Raymond" Len put his hand out to Raymond and they shake hands.

"What do you want the Ritz for? When you have all you need here…a friendly ear to get rid of all your problems" Raymond says with pride and a little smugness, he was clearly hurt from what and how John had spoken.

"You know John when I broke up with Annie, you remember don't you? How broken down I was, how I wondered what went wrong? You said don't worry about it, and that I would get back on my feet in no time"

"Well its different isn't it I have lost my home and wife"

Len jumped in and snaps out "Annie was my wife! And I had kids as well…not just the fucking house that I had worked so bloody hard for, I lost it all and took nothing from Annie or the kids, so that Annie and the kids could…could have somewhere…" just then John interrupted

"Yes I know… sorry I guess I'm feeling sorry for myself"

"Raymond do you remember when I arrived, all those years ago, just a bag of clothes, and how broken I was, I could not work out for the life of me what had happened"

"Yes I remember… but I told you that the truth had a way of coming out or finding a way out, the truth would come out one day and…"

Raymond stops and looks at John in a distrustful way.

"Well I would like to know the truth, what the hell has gone wrong with my life? And more importantly what the hell has gone on for Jan to have behaved the way she has, she won't even answer any of my bloody calls or return any of my text message"

"Be careful John for what you ask, the truth might come and kick you… even harder than it has all ready, you might be better just leaving it as it is…" John interrupts and stops Len carrying on.

"What the hell have I done to deserve this? I have been a good husband; I never hurt anyone, what the fuck has gone wrong! What the hell has gotten into her?"

Len turns and looks at Raymond, Raymond nods his head.

"Go on put him out of his misery"

"Do you know something? Len tell me (*John grabs hold of Lens arms shaking him*) tell me! Fucking tell me what has gone on. (*Still holding Lens arms*) tell me man"

Len pushes John off him, and pushes him down on the chair behind him. "Get the hell off me! You want to know… Do you? Well I've got a tale to tell you, (*poking John in his chest)* and it goes back fifteen years, if not longer"

"WHAT! This is an old vendetta? Not you is it…don't tell me it's you, no not you. WHY? What have I ever done to you! I don't believe it it's not you…tell me it's not you!"

"I'll tell you the story, then you will know who and why"

"Do you want to take this upstairs? Or would you prefer me to stop here? And keep things in some sort of order"

"What do you think?" John asked looking up at Len

"Raymond you've been a good friend of mine for a good number of years, and a good judge of character, I'll leave the decision in your hands; do as you think is right"

"Well maybe you should go upstairs, as I might be having some people coming around, but I will pop up every now and again, just to make sure that all is well, OK? After all you both have a lot to talk about"

"Yes that's ok with me; we'll go up to my room ok Len"

"Ok but Ray… you know how I would like things; no! We're going to the room just above here"

"Yes Len I know what you want, and yes you can use the room above this one" John and Len leave the room. Not much longer there is a knock on Raymond's front door, Raymond gets up and goes to answer the door, he then comes back into his room with Sally.

Chapter 10

"ARE THEY UPSTAIRS?" Sally asked as she took her coat off and pulled up a chair.

"Yes, they've not long gone up, a few moments earlier you would have walked into them, what time is Wayne coming around?"

"He said he would be here, I thought he would or was here already, that's why I came a little earlier than we had arranged"

"Well I'm sure he won't be much longer, do you want a drink Sally? I have your favourite, went to the shops myself for it, it's in the top cupboard on the left hand side"

"Yes please (*as she puckers up to Raymond*) I don't need to know where it is do I? I'm not making it am I?"

"You can stop doing that (*he says as he flicks her bottom with a towel that was over a chair, Sally runs around the chair trying to get away from him, just then there is a knock at the door*) I bet you want me to answer it"

"That will be Wayne" she says as she is puffing and panting, as Raymond goes to answer the door she blows him a kiss.

Raymond and Wayne come in laughing and carrying on.

"What's the joke?" Sally asks still panting a little.

"Just something Ray said"

"What?"

"Just the look on John's face when he sees Ray changed"

Raymond goes out of the room to get changed,

"What do you think will happen? When we all go and see them together"

"Well I suspected that Len has laid the groundwork and John should be…in denial…or…what's the right word?"

Sally interrupts Wayne. "Do you think he'll be violent?"

"Who?"

"John who do you think? Not Len he's a gentlemen"

"No! At least I hope not"

"You're a softy" she says as she's running around the chairs teasing Wayne, with her top buttons open and she wiggles her chest at Wayne.

"NO I am not a softy! It's just the …"

"The look on your face when I said that, you're a softy"

"Stop or I'll put you over my knee"

"You and who's army? (*Still being seductive panting puckering her lips, Raymond comes back. He has a smart suit on and his hair is tidy, he turns the radio off*) Come over here you beast (*Raymond stands and looks at her, Sally runs towards Raymond and jumps around his waist, wrapping her legs around him and kisses him on the lips*) have you ever seen anyone so sexy" she says looking at Wayne blowing him a kiss.

"He's not my type, how long?"

Sally interrupts "mind your own business you naughty man"

"You stop being silly Sally, how long will we give them before we go up and see them?"

"Sally will go up first, then we'll stand at the door just in case"

"You don't think he'll hurt her do you?" Wayne asks with a shaky voice.

"He has had everything taken away from him, who knows how he will react. Being ex army and a number of other things who knows what he'll do?"

"I'll just put my charm on, and he'll be putty in my hands (*purring*) like most men and women" she says rubbing her finger down Wayne's cheek.

There is a loud bang from upstairs and a lot of shouting, then a deadly silence.

"Do you think its time for us to go?" Sally asked with a worried look on her face.

"No! They will just be getting acquainted" Raymond says as he laughs.

Wayne sits down and picks up the newspaper; Sally goes behind Wayne and massages his shoulders. Raymond goes off into the Kitchen.

"Do you like that?" Sally says long and slowly almost purring.

"Yes it's lovely" he holds her hand then turns his head and kissed her on the cheek.

"Do you think we should go upstairs?"

"Not really, I think we should let Len and John just sort it out, I don't see what we have to gain going up, I don't know whose idea it was but I see no point in us looking bad"

"Wayne you're a right softy, you're frightened of your own shadow; I've never known anyone like you" Sally then squeezes Wayne's cheek, and plants another kiss on his lips.

Chapter 11

BACK IN THE UPSTAIRS room, John is sitting on the edge of the bed, Len is walking around. Len could clearly see that John was anxious, so he was somewhat unsure if he should start the story or just leave it well alone. After some time he thought that he had waited long enough, so he started the conversation; he was still unsure but he knew that it had to come out, once he started he would not be able to hold anything back.

"Right it goes back years" Len said still a little apprehensive on how John might react.

"What does?"

"The story that I'm going to tell you!" he says with anger in his voce almost snarling.

"Get on with it then" John says with almost contempt waving his hand.

Len stands looks at John and shakes his head; he then picks up the clock "you've had this some time now"

"Yes it was grandad's"

"I know (*he puts the clock down*) you might not remember when me and Annie broke up"

"Annie and I"

"What?"

"It's bad grammar, me and Annie, the right way is Annie and I"

"Well ok! What fucking ever…at times you're a fucking arsehole! Getting back to the fucking story, when we broke up, you recall I had no idea why"

"You said you had no idea. It's a shit hole this, what made you tell me about this place?"

"It's where I came, when I broke up with Annie"

"She took everything" John says in a sad voice

"What?"

"Jan, she took everything, she said if I give her it all, without a fight, she would not push the fact that I had an affair with a client"

"So why give up?"

"I would never work again, I would have lost my licence, at least I can still work this way"

"With your detective skills, you will find out who and why"

"Yes! And when I do there will be hell to pay"

"What? …why would anyone do this to you John?"

"I've thought about this and I cannot work out why, I've done nothing wrong to anyone that I can think off, nothing at all"

"Well anyway getting on, I came across something not too long ago, and it became clear why Annie threw me out"

"Why was that then?"

"I was given some old photos"

"Right…what photos? by whom?" John was now looking uncomfortable.

"It was my son Tony, on his eighteenth birthday"

"So you've got together with him at last, well done"

"He came knocking at my house late one night, when I opened the door I was punched to the floor, then photos thrown on me and then told that for his birthday he had just buried his mum" Len then takes out some photos from his pocket and throws them at John.

"What are you playing at?" Picking the photos up, he then looks at them, his face worried.
"He had been going through her stuff, through Annie's stuff and came across the photos, and as you can see they tell a story…WHY JOHN! Why?"

"I can explain!" Len goes across to John and puts his hands around Johns neck and strangles him, John falls to the floor, Len lets go of him, he then picks the photos up and stands looking at them, he then placing them in some sort of order in his hand.

"Yes I bet you can" John sits back down on the chair. Len was still pacing the floor. He was still looking at the photos, still placing them in some sort of order.

John was now was looking a little arrogant as he was tucking his shirt back into his trousers. He then stood up putting his collar right.
"No good looking untidy is it" he says as he looks Len up and down.

Chapter 12

SALLY TURNED THE radio on, Duffy's song Mercy is playing. Sally starts to sing to the song, and starts to play the part with a seductive dance routine towards Wayne, who is looking uneasy. This makes Sally flirt even more, and more seductive towards Wayne.

"Yeah, yeah, yeah…Yeah, yeah, yeah… Yeah, yeah, yeah…Yeah, yeah, yeah, I love you…But I gotta stay true …My morals got me on my knees… I'm begging please, Stop playing games…I don't know what this is.
'Cos you got me good, just like you knew you would I don't know what you do? But you do it so well I'm under your spell

You got me begging you for mercy…Why won't you release me
You got me begging you for mercy…Why won't you release me
I said release me!

She jumps on his lap stroking his hair looking into his eyes.
"Now you think that I will be something on the side. But you got to understand…That I need a man who can take my hands yes I do"

I don't know what this is but you got me good"

The dance routine lasts for approximately 2-3min, Then Raymond returns into the room carrying a cup, then turns the radio off

"You been making a cuppa and not us one" Sally asks with a smile

"You been making a cuppa and not making us one? (*mimicking Sally*) Yours are in the kitchen" Wayne gets up and goes into the kitchen

"When do you think we should go up and see them two? There has been a lot of noise coming from up there" Sally asks with a little concern.

"I think we will have a drink then I will go up…then Wayne then you" Wayne enters with the drinks giving Sally hers

"Wayne will do what?" Wayne asks with a worried look on his face.

"Go up and sort those two out" Raymond says laughing. Sally and Raymond both laugh at Wayne's look of surprise.

"I don't think that's a good idea" Wayne says with a shaky voice.

"Why not? Raymond asks slightly sternly.

"Well … well …well its just not"

Sally joins in on Raymond's fun, twisting and wiggling her leg, one over the over "well I just love a man, who likes to get involved with a bust up"

"A bust up! Not me I'm not in this not for any bust ups, that was never on the cards"

"Then Sally its back to you (*he winks at Sally*) there's no way that I'm going up and sorting them two out" Raymond nod's to Sally, then his eyes looking in the direction of Wayne.

"Call yourself men, well I will go and sort them out, then I'm going to find me a real man"

"Tell you what! I haven't thought this out properly, let's have a think first" Raymond says rubbing his chin as if he was thinking.

"What do you mean?" Wayne asked hoping that Raymond has thought of a better idea not involving him.

"We could go up there, and all hell might break out, no I haven't thought this one out at all (*he sits down near Sally*) no I haven't thought it out proper after all it does at times sound a bit lively up there"

"Maybe we should call one of them down here first. To see how it's going, and take it from there? At least that way they are separated for a while" Sally says, thinking that it does sound at times far worse than any of them had imagined it would be.

Raymond starts to laugh "I'll go up first, don't worry I'm just winding you two up, I always was going to go first"

"Sally do you want any biscuits with your cuppa? If Raymond's going up there we might as well have a biscuit, is that's ok Raymond?"

Raymond looks at Wayne and shakes his head "you're something else, yes take what you want"

"Wayne ever the gentleman, no you're all right, I think we best start getting ready to go and see them two upstairs, Wayne you as well as Raymond"

Wayne's face is in bewilderment, the idea of going upstairs,   Raymond starts to laugh, and Sally starts as well.

Raymond still laughing "The look on your face, Wayne you're a one off"

"What? What do you mean a one off...one off what?"

"Never mind, Raymond is going up first, he is going to get dressed back up in those old clothes, and we'll stay here out of harms way"

"I would have gone up first, you know that...it's just I think we should play this out carefully that's all. Anyway what is Raymond putting his old cloths back on for?"

"Just to get back into character I think? He wanted to put his normal clothes on but when he did he said that he didn't feel right for the part. Or something like that"

Chapter 13

JOHN AND LEN are still in the room, they have calmed down a little and Len's wanting answers to his questions, John is arrogantly more than happy to answer.

"Look at those photos what picture do they tell you? What would you think after been given them?"

"They look convincing enough, you can understand why she throw you out, even now looking at them it tells the story of what a rotten two timing bast…"

Len stopped him finishing his sentence "I sat many a night looking at them, the harder I looked, then one night it all became clear"

"What became clear?"

"Look at this one, me kissing that girl, (*he picks one out and shows John*) do you see who it is?"

"Not really"

"It's Karen, I was meant to meet you for a night out, you never turned up, Karen said that she had seen you a week earlier, and told you that she was having a hen's night or leaving do, before she moved a way to get married to Brian who was living abroad"

"So what does this prove? It's a long time ago how the hell do you think I'm going to remember something as trivial as a night out, come on man get to fucking grips with reality"

Len pulls another photo out "This one look at it, a different angle but it looks like Karen"

"Yes I see what you mean"

"They are all the same, but the thing is the only one that is clear is the one of me kissing Karen on that night out, me kissing her goodbye and wishing her luck"

"But they do look like you, I mean to say (*picking one)* look at this one, you might not see your face or hers but it does look like you"

"That's what it looks like, you're right, but I know it wasn't me, it's not me, so I tried to work out who it might be, why would someone want to break Annie and me up"

"Anyway what fucking clever dick conclusion did you come too?"

"Annie never married again, and as you know I never did. So I would guess that she loved me as much as I loved her"

"I'm sorry for you Len really sorry for you" John gets up and moves around the room with a look of sympathy for Len.

"Fifteen years"

"What?"

"Fifteen years we could have had together (*turning away from John)* if some rotten jealous bastard kept his sickness to himself"

"Calm down …calm down Len, what has this got to do with me?"

"IT WAS YOU!"

"What?"

"YOU…it took me three years after getting the photos, to workout who it was, and do you know what? it was staring me in the face all the time"

"How do you work that out?" John starts getting all defensive.

"This photo (*pulling out the last photo*) this one" he hands it to John.

"I don't see how you can make out anything in this, all you can see is two naked people but you can't see the faces"

"No you're right, no faces on any of the photos all but that ONE… me kissing Karen goodbye, on her night out…the night out that you were supposed to be at, the one that you had arranged"

"Well Sherlock I don't see how you can work that out (*looking at the photo*) by this one picture" John tosses it down with the other photos on the bed.

"NO!"

"NO, how the hell can YOU stand blaming me for a terrible thing and only on this" picking it back up and shoving it forward

"THIS!" Picking up the travel clock

"What?"

"This gave you away. Grandad's clock"

"What? What the…"

"I know how much, this means to you, and it goes where you go, SO WHY...WHY DID you take my happiness away?" Len sits on the bed looking and feeling exhausted.

"It was me who had the education, it was me in the army, it was me who had a scholarship, it was me who had the elegant wife, it was...me who couldn't have children, YES... YES I WAS ENVIOUS jealous, what ever you want to fucking call it"

"You took away Annie and the kids' happiness, just because you thought that we were, or had something you didn't have"

"So you are behind this, me losing my home business... that's just as bad, even worse"

"NO! No its not, the photos showed that you have played away, and that you are untrustworthy, you're the worst scheming pitiful bastard that I know, and Jan has seen this for herself, if I was to show her this, do you think that she would let you keep your P I licence?"

"You rotten bastard!"

"ME you took all my happiness away, to think I could have had the last fifteen years with Annie, and you took all that away"

John stands up, Len lunges at him they wrestle, they fall to the ground punching each other John on top of Len then Len rolls over and somehow gets on top of John. They punch each other, kick each other when they could, the door opens, in comes Raymond and he splits the two of them up.

Raymond tells Len to go into his old room that he used once; Len puts his clothes right and tucks himself in, he gives

John a look that would frighten almost anyone, a look of anger and aggression.

"No I'm ok I'll stay (*Raymond turns and looks at Len*) no sorry Ray I'm done honest I'm done, you'll get no more out of me honest"

John gets up ready to fight again; Len stands his ground looking squarely into John's eyes, shown no sign of fear.

Raymond jumps up in-between the two again "Look you two stop right now! You should think yourself lucky that your brother got you this room"

"What? You're fucking kidding aren't you?"

"Well now I know what type of bloke you are, (*he says picking John's belongings up*) you can take yourself and piss off, I never thought I was particular until I met you (*Then he throw's Johns bag at him*) and if I see you on the street I will spit on you, you're scum, Now go and get out you bloody piece of shit"

John stands at the door looking at the two of them, Len and Raymond stand looking at him, hoping that he will go without anymore disturbance. Sally and Wayne enter, passing John in the doorway, Len sits on the bed Raymond standing near him.

"Are you two alright? we heard the racket downstairs and thought that we should come up and make sure that you are all ok"

"Thanks Sally but I think Len needs a moment by himself, (*Raymond moves towards the door and looks along the corridor and down the staircase he couldn't see John*) Right I think he's gone there should be no more trouble" they head back down to

Raymond's room leaving Len sitting on the bed alone, his head in his hands thinking what had happened thinking how bad he has felt, how bad he has been, as bad as John.

Chapter 14

RAYMOND PUTS THE kettle on almost straight away as they enter the room, Wayne and Sally sit on the chairs near the small table made for four.

"It sounded terrible up there Ray"

"It was for a while, I walked in on them fighting I thought that they were going to kill each other"

"Do you think we have done the right thing?" Wayne asked in a timid way.

"Yes we've done the right thing, after what that John has done! (*Shakes her head*) he's done far worse than we have"

"I can't help feel bad for what I have done, I feel sorry that we have done this, its not nice; we maybe should have left it alone" Sally moves over to Wayne and grasped hold of his cheeks.

"It's good that you feel bad, it shows that you're a decent bloke, and not a scheming bastard! Like that John" then she kisses him on the lips.

Raymond comes in from the kitchen with three cups of tea, he could hear what was being said, so didn't say anything. Sally seemed to have it as it should be he thought.

"Raymond how did you meet Len? You two are a million times different in so many ways" Sally asks as she takes her cup from Raymond.

Raymond took a drink he was in deep thought, then it was as if the light had turned on. He started to tell Sally and Wayne how Len had first came to stay there.

"It was late one night, the weather hadn't been the best, I had lived here for almost all my life, my mother and father had this as a bed and breakfast when the factories were all over in this area. Anyway when they died, my parents, it wasn't long after that that the factory's started to shut"

Sally and Wayne almost at the same time asked what happened to the factories.

"I'm not really sure to be honest, they just started to shut, those who had worked in some of them stayed here, there were pubs and bars all over in this area, and the factories which brought workers in from all over"

"Must have been great in those days plenty going on, loads of work" As Wayne said this Raymond and Sally looked at each other, almost pulling the same face as if he had a day's work in him. They started to laugh.

"Anyway getting back to Len, I was pulling up outside one night if I remember right, I had been somewhere, anyway I saw this dark shadow around the side of the house it…he was fallen down. Like I said the weather wasn't that good, at first I thought…well I don't know what I thought. I went to see what was happing"

"Weren't you scared?"

"Well yes Wayne I suppose I was, anyway I went around to see what was going on, was he a drunk or a druggie sort, even if the house looked a little shabby I don't want those sort making it any worse than it was or is. After all it's my house"

I looked at him, I looked at him in his eyes, it was as if he had given up, I mean I've never seen anyone like that before,

I've seen down and out's but they …he looked like all he wanted was to lie-down and die"

"How sad…but you got him back on his feet"

"Yes I did Sally, it took a long time, he told me about his wife and how she kicked him out for no reason, then when he went to pick up the kids she was sometimes there, if looks could kill, anyway it was getting hard for him, he loved her I mean he really loved her (*he stopped to get his thoughts and a breath, then carried on with the story*) So I advised him maybe not to see her, if it was hurting him every time he seen her… I told him too avoid her, he then arranged to get the kids from the end of the street where he lived. As much as he loved having the kids he couldn't stop asking about his wife. They would tell him she was having fun, …I think it all got to much then she slowly had things happing… appointments when Len was supposed to have them then it slowly became easer just to cut his loss and walk away (*Sally moved to another chair so that she could hear better, Raymond was starting to speak a little quieter, she could see that it brought some sad memories back for Raymond*) I'm not sure? I suppose at the time it did help him, I was going to a drama school. I asked him if he wanted to come I mean it was only amateur dramatics"

"Why did you give him the worst room in the house … I mean to say it's a pigsty"

"Sally you wouldn't believe me, he picked that room even when he got back onto his feet he wouldn't give it up, it took ages before he finally moved out, he said what ever he had done to his wife and kids this was his payment. Or punishment"

"Did you believe him when he said that he hadn't done anything to hurt his wife, I mean to say you must have thought that he had played away or something? He's a good looking guy"

"Sally…Sally…well I suppose so at first, but do you know what and I mean this when we had night's out he sometimes got chatting with women, sometimes they would give him their number, as far as I know and am aware of he never, even after all this time, had an affair with anyone, so no I don't think he did, well we know now he didn't"

"How can someone do that sort of thing to his brother? And not have any remorse, I couldn't do that, I feel guilty doing what we've done, (*Sally and Ray looked at him*) Don't get me wrong I know he's done some bad things but …" he couldn't finish what he wanted to say he couldn't find the right words.

"It all catches you up sooner or later, and pay back is not always the same as the deed that has been done, jealousy is a bad thing, the green-eyed monster has been the route too many a bad journey, just as John has found out"

"I suppose you're right Sally, his wife never strayed, not even when we tried to get her off with Frank. (*He laughs*) That was a dint in Franks armour, he looked right huffed about that, thought he could get off with anyone" they all laugh

"There you see, what goes around comes around"

"I feel sorry for Jan"

"Why?" Sally asked as she was taking a drink

"Well she is the innocent party here, she seemed a lovely woman"

"Well on that note, we've done her a favour, getting that big, cheating, lying, scum of the earth out of her life, haven't we?"

All of a sudden there's a loud banging from upstairs another fight has started Sally was the first up and out the room followed by Raymond then Wayne, Sally was up the stairs taking two at a time, Raymond not as much but still faster than Wayne.

Sally got to the doorway of the room she could see John on top of Len, she could only see Len's feet at the bottom of the bed. He was struggling, then John hit him with something, there was a loud thud then again another thud. Lens feet stopped moving, then John pulled something from out of his jacket, there was no sound but a squirt of blood like a fountain pen, squirting up onto Johns white shirt and jacket and some onto his chin. John then got up and calmly walked passed Sally who was now screaming with fear. He looked her up and down and said in the coldest way possible.

"How did you think it was going to end?"

Then walked passed Raymond then Wayne, who looked at John. The colour drained from Wayne's face then he fell to the floor, this was too much for all of them.

Raymond ran into the room he tried to help Len but it was too late. Sally heard the front door shut ever so quietly; not a slam as she was expecting, but calmly and quietly the monster was gone.

Printed in Poland
by Amazon Fulfillment
Poland Sp. z o.o., Wrocław

62203224R00035